Harry Clever Spider at School

Written by Julia Jarman
Illustrated by Charlie Fowkes

Harry was Clare's pet spider and he was very clever.
Clare wanted to show Harry to all her friends.
On Monday she took him to school.
"We're doing minibeasts," she told him.
"This box is just for the journey."

But Harry didn't like his box. He hid in the corner so that Clare couldn't see him.

Harry was still hiding when they got to school. Joanne said, "I've got ever such a big black beetle. Look!"

Simon said, "I've got an enormous furry caterpillar that will turn into a brilliant butterfly. Look!"

Clare said, "I've got a huge, hairy, clever spider. Look!"

Joanne looked through one of the holes in the box and said, "I can't see him."

No one could see Harry.
"Wait till we get inside," said Clare.
"You'll see him when I take the lid off."

But when they got inside, their teacher, Miss Bradley, said, "Keep your minibeasts in their jars and boxes, children. Don't remove the lids.
We can't have minibeasts running all over the classroom, can we?"

She gave out paper and pencils and put out the paint pots.
"Please observe your minibeast carefully. Then write about what you see. After that, you can draw or paint a picture of it."

Clare looked through the holes in the lid of Harry's box, but she still couldn't see him.

She said, "Please Miss Bradley, I can't see Harry with the lid on."

But Miss Bradley wasn't listening.
She had lost her glasses.
She was always losing them!
She said, "Get on with your work everyone, while I look for my glasses."

Clare opened the lid to peep at Harry, who jumped out ...
... and scuttled away!

Clare had never seen him move so fast.

"See," said Joanne, looking into the box.
"It's empty."
"You were fibbing," said Simon. "You haven't got a clever spider. You haven't got a spider at all!"

Clare was upset. Where was Harry?
Miss Bradley was upset.
Where were her glasses?
She said, "I can't see without my glasses.
Children, please help me look for them."

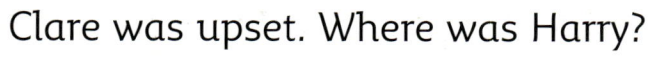

Everybody started looking for Miss Bradley's glasses, except Clare.
She was looking for Harry.

She looked on her table.
"There he is!"
But it was a splash of black paint.

She looked on the next table.
"There he is!"
But it was another splash of black paint.

Then Clare looked again, more closely.
She saw a trail …
… leading down the table leg,
across the floor and up the wall,
to the ceiling.

"There's Harry!" yelled Clare. "There's my clever spider!"

Everybody was looking at Harry.
Miss Bradley was furious.
"Clare, I told you to keep your minibeast INSIDE its box!"
Clare said, "Sorry, Miss Bradley, but I think Harry's seen something."

Harry was bungee jumping.
Down he went ... then up again, just like a yo-yo.
Then he went down behind the cupboard.
Harry *had* seen something ...

... Miss Bradley's glasses!

"You really are a clever spider," said Miss Bradley.

"He's *very* clever," said Clare. "Look at him now."

Very Clever Spider

What Harry can do

Harry can hide.

Harry can bungee jump.

Harry can write.

Ideas for guided reading

Learning objectives: tell real and imagined stories using the conventions of familiar story language; read independently and with increasing fluency longer and less familiar texts; use syntax and context to build their store of vocabulary when reading for meaning; explain their reactions to texts, commenting on important aspects; word process short non narrative texts

Curriculum links: Science: Living things in the environment

Interest words: minibeast, journey, caterpillar, butterfly, observe, scuttled, ceiling, bungee

Resources: non-fiction books about minibeasts

Word count: 507

Getting started

- Ask the children to read the covers independently and predict what will happen.
- Read through the interest words together and check they are familiar with them.
- Demonstrate reading pp2–3 and ask the children to predict what will happen next.
- Read pp4–5 together, prompting and praising recognition of the interest words.

Reading and responding

- Listen to each child read in turn as the others read independently. Prompt and praise use of phonic clues to decode new words.
- Stop at p11 and discuss how Clare felt when Simon told her she was fibbing. Ask the children to think of times when they might not have been believed. How did they feel?
- Ask the children to read to the end independently. Were their initial predictions about how the story ends correct?